The Day the Spaceship Landed

by Beman Lord

pictures by Harold Berson

New York   HENRY Z. WALCK, INC.

To HZW

Contents

1. Visitors from Space

My name is Michael Davis and people call me Mike, naturally. One thing I really like is frogs' legs. You have got to catch the grandfathers because they're the best. They have more meat on their legs than the little ones. All through school that day I couldn't get the smell or taste out of my head. I couldn't answer a single question Miss Rose, my teacher, asked me.

"Mike," she said, "are you with us today?"

"Yes," I answered. It was easier to say yes than explain. Miss Rose came from a big city and probably had never smelled frogs' legs frying on the stove.

Anyway, school finally got out, and I raced home to change my clothes. About a half mile from our house is a swamp which is where I catch the frogs. Sometimes, after a good rain, it is pretty wet in there, but most times it just has scattered ponds. Afternoon is the best time to catch the frogs, because they have been sunning themselves and are a little groggy. They can't move fast. Well, I changed, took a shopping bag, and started for the swamp.

Some people, I suppose, could get lost in there. It really isn't that big, and I know my way around. My plan was to head for the center, but I checked a few ponds on the way. I didn't have too much time, since it gets dark early this time of year. I came out of the bushes, and then I saw it. At the same time it saw me. It was a space saucer. I felt a tingling go through my body.

"Don't be alarmed," a voice said. "You have been frozen to the spot."

I didn't know whether that tingling was the freeze or my excitement. I just looked.

"We will release you in a minute," the voice continued. "The area will be decontrolled as soon as we adjust our equipment. Do not be afraid. We will not hurt you."

I wasn't too sure about that and tried to move, but found they were right. I couldn't move.

The spaceship or saucer was round and about twenty feet in diameter. It looked like it was made of aluminum or some shiny metal. It was smooth all over. As I looked at it I felt another tingle, and suddenly a door slid open. Four men came out. They looked just like what I thought spacemen should look like. Spacesuits and helmets.

"Bonjour," one said.

"Buenos días," one said.

"Zdravstvouité," one said.

"Hello," one said.

"Hello," I answered rather weakly, and found I could move.

"You speak English. As you can see, we were prepared for French, Spanish or Russian —and other languages too. Two days before

landing, our directional finder and communications system went out of order, and we were not sure where we would land. Let me introduce us. I am 132D. This is 632X, 515A and 804CC.

"My name is Michael Davis but people call me Mike," I said.

"You are a boy," one of the numbers said. "Is that correct?"

"Yes," I said laughingly. "I'm ten years old. Where are you from?"

"Our planet is called Barko. It is of the Nark group. It was their joint effort which sent us here. We really had not planned to land but were to concentrate only on gathering information. When repairs were necessary, we had no choice. Is there a war going on here?"

"No," I said, "not here, but overseas."

"Before we lost reception, we heard about wars. Also our television picked up a lot of men calling each other names. They each kept saying, 'When I am in power...'"

"We are going to have elections. That always happens," I said, and they looked puzzled. "Every few years we change governments and elect new people to run things. How do you breathe?"

One of the other men spoke up. I just couldn't remember their numbers. "We breathe carbon dioxide. We separate it from the atmosphere."

"Boy, that would kill us. You probably know, we breathe oxygen," I said. "Can we sit down? I've got a lot of questions."

"Will you be missed?" one asked. "It is getting rather dark."

"Holy smoke. It is." I hadn't even noticed it. "Yes. We have a strict rule in our house—be on time for meals. I'll have to do a lot of explaining."

"I'm afraid that will be out of the question. You will be blocked from speaking or writing anything about us. When we leave in a few days, you will be unblocked. Understand? Naturally, we have many questions to ask you. You will find your way back here. Do you have school tomorrow?"

"We sure do. This is only Wednesday. I'll be here right after, though."

"We are quite sure of that. Now you had better hurry home."

"Okay, I'll see you tomorrow afternoon."

I made it home in ten minutes flat, but I was too late. Everybody was at the table.

"Where have you been?" my father asked. "You know the supper hours."

"I'm sorry I'm late," I said, "but wait until you hear what I've seen."

"We are waiting," Dad said slowly.

"I saw..." I couldn't say anything, and then I remembered about my mind being blocked.

"Hurry up with it," Dad said. "We're waiting for the explanation."

How could I explain? I could see my father getting angrier and angrier. He picked up his water glass and started to bring it to his lips. Halfway there, something happened. The glass slipped and water went everywhere.

"I'll wipe it up," Mom said, jumping up from her chair. "Mike, take your plate of food and go in the kitchen. Immediately."

I filled my plate and went to the kitchen table. That was the rule of the house. When you are late, you eat in the kitchen. I sat there thinking. That was a funny thing about the water spilling. My father never spills. Also I wondered what *they* were eating.

2. Blocked in Space

The morning at school went very slowly. How can you do math and think about a spaceship? I wasn't too hungry at lunchtime, but managed to eat three ice creams and two pieces of cherry pie. My first class in the afternoon was gym, and I played a fair game of touch football. It was the second class that caused the trouble.

"I thought this afternoon we would do creative writing," Miss Rose said. "You may either write a story or a poem. I think I've picked a very interesting subject, one that you will all be interested in, I'm sure. It is, 'The Day the Spaceship Landed.'"

Several kids said, "What a great subject."

My mind had been blocked from saying anything about the saucer, but could I write about a spaceship — or were they the same thing?

"You will have a half to three quarters of an hour to write," Miss Rose continued.

I took out paper and pencil and was nervous about beginning. Betty Miller, the girl in front of me, and Steve Mackay, the boy across the way, had already started.

"Don't think too long about it," Miss Rose said to the class, but looking at me.

I tried to write "The Day the Spaceship Landed." The only thing I got on the paper was "The Day the." Miss Rose looked at me again. Hurriedly I wrote the first thing that came in my head. It was...."I'm blocked, all right." I wrote that sentence on both sides of the paper.

"All right. Time is up," Miss Rose said. "Please read Chapter 7 in *Exploring Science* while I look at your papers."

I got through two pages before Miss Rose called me to her desk.

"What is the meaning of this?" she asked. "I hardly call this creative writing."

"I can't write about that subject," I said.

"That is hardly an excuse. I have seen some of your papers with flying saucers and spaceships on them so I know that this interests you. Finish your reading, and then you'll spend some time with me after school, until you finish your assignment."

"I can't. I have an appointment with some people," I said.

"That will have to wait. Please take your seat."

I read the chapter but couldn't remember anything I read. All I could think of was what 804CC or 632X had said. It was something about being sure I would be back. Did they have control of me as well as blocking my mind?

After school I sat for about five minutes with pencil in hand. I was getting nervous. Then the phone rang, and Miss Rose answered it.

"That was the principal. There is going to be a special teachers' meeting right away. I will have to excuse you. Tomorrow is Halloween, so I don't want to keep you then. That means I'll expect the composition the first thing Monday morning."

"Thanks, Miss Rose," I said. "Monday will be fine. I'll be able to write then and also talk."

She looked at me with surprise. I quickly got my jacket, picked up my books, and fled. That sure was a lucky break about the principal calling a meeting. I started to wonder more about it and then thought I had better get home and change my clothes. Suddenly I felt

myself drawn toward the swamp. I ran faster. They were waiting for me.

"I'm sorry I'm late. I had to stay after school because..."

One of them interrupted me, "We know. That was why we had you come here before changing your clothes. We don't have too much time, and besides we don't want to make you late for dinner again tonight." He smiled through his glass helmet.

"I've gotten into some jams because I can't say anything about you," I said.

"Don't be too upset. You'll be able to explain when we leave. You really are protecting us. We will be back in two years on an official visit. Do you suppose you could get us some samples of food and clothing? We have gathered soil, rocks, plants and so on."

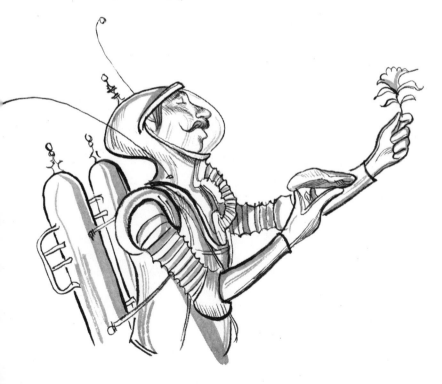

"Sure," I said. "By the way, can you eat our food? I thought of that last night at supper."

"We take pills. I believe we could drink your water after taking out some of the oxygen, but our scientists would have to test it before we did. Now, we have listed some questions we hope you will answer. We think we have the answers but would like to check our findings."

"I'll try," I said. "You know, I'm only in the fifth grade. I don't know everything."

They then proceeded to ask the questions. They were not hard to answer. Planets in our solar system and their descriptions, type of weather and stuff like that.

"These aren't hard questions at all. Why

don't I leave my books here, and you can study them. I will need them for school tomorrow, though."

"You can have them back tonight when you bring us the food and clothing. It will only take our copier an hour or so to photograph them. Now you'd better run, and we'll see you after supper."

"Could you meet me at the edge of the swamp? This place gets pretty spooky at night. I'm not afraid, but I might get lost."

"One of us will be at the edge. He'll see that you find him."

I ate with the family that night. Mom asked me where I had been all afternoon, and I said I had to stay after school. Fortunately the phone rang, and I didn't have to explain why. I wouldn't have been able to, anyway.

After supper I went up to my room and hunted for old clothes. I wasn't sure I was going to get the things back. The folks would be pleased at the way I cleaned my room. I got rid of that old holey sweater Mom had been trying to throw out, two ties that my dad said didn't go with anything, a torn handkerchief, and lots of old things. I tied them in a ball and went down to the kitchen.

The dishwasher was going, so I knew the coast was clear. I got out some plastic bags so everything wouldn't be a mess. I took a little bit of each leftover—two slices of bread, an orange, celery, pickles, one egg and other stuff. I even took some hot mustard. I sure

would like to see their faces when they tasted that! I got everything nicely gathered and was about to leave when Mom came in.

"Are you going on a picnic or leaving home?" she asked.

"Nothing like that," I said. "You see I have been asked to gather some things for..." I

was blocked and had to come up with a quick answer. "...for the Halloween party."

"Oh," she said, not sure whether to believe me or not.

"Can I explain in a few days?" I asked slowly.

She threw up her hands, and I grabbed a flashlight and beat it out the back door.

3. Witch from Outer Space

All four of them were waiting for me when I reached the edge of the swamp.

"How did you know I would come here?" I asked.

They smiled. One of them said, "We knew. I see you have brought the things. Thank you."

I handed over the bundles. "I can't stay too long. My folks don't like me to stay out too late on a weekday."

"Here are your books. Tomorrow when you come, could you bring us a map of your planet?"

"We are having a Halloween party and parade tomorrow." They looked puzzled. "Everybody gets dressed up and wears masks so they don't know who you are. They award prizes for the best costumes. I'm going as a hobo, and I haven't got it ready yet. Could I

skip tomorrow and come first thing Saturday morning?"

"That will shorten our time with you. We are planning to leave Saturday night."

"Why doesn't one of you come with me? You've got great costumes."

"That would be a wonderful chance to see the village," one said. He turned to the others.

"Do you think it would be safe for one of us to go?"

"Excuse me," I said. "Your heads are a little bigger than ours, but I could get a big mask to go over that. No one would spot you then."

They looked at each other. "We are willing to take the risk and will decide later which one of us will go. I think probably 515A, because he is your height."

"Great! You'll have a good time," I said to the whole group, as I sure didn't know which one was 515A. "I'll drop the map and mask at the ship on my way home from school. You probably will need some time to get it fixed under your helmet. Then I'll pick you up right after supper. The parade starts at seven."

They all nodded. We said good-by, and I

ran home. Thank goodness I had a flashlight.

The next day I talked the librarian into letting me take an atlas home over the week-end. They don't usually go out of the library, but she let me do it just this time if I would bring it back first thing Monday morning. I also stopped and bought a mask at the five and dime. I got a witch one because it had a long face with a big pointed hat. That would surely cover his head. They must have more brains that we do, I thought.

They were pleased with the atlas and said they could get it all copied by night. The mask made them all laugh. I still didn't know which one was going to the party. They got rid of me pretty fast, and I think they were all going to try on the mask as soon as I left.

I fixed up my costume before supper. I didn't eat much, because I was pretty excited. Who else has ever gone to a Halloween party with a *real* spaceman?

When I got to the swamp one of them was waiting. "I still can't remember your numbers," I said, "but tonight I had better call you by a name. We don't have numbers down here. How about Bill?"

"Fine," he said. "My orders are to stick right with you."

"Okay, Bill," I said. "Remember my name is Mike. Let's go."

The parade was to form by the bandstand on the green. We were to walk around the square once, and then past the judges' stand on the Methodist Church steps. After the judging, the party was going to be held in the church.

There were a lot of children there when we arrived.

A clown came up to us and looked at the spaceman. "What a great costume," he yelled.

It was Steve Mackay. I could tell by his voice. "Don't touch him. You'll ruin his costume." I had to get rid of him. I did not want anybody examining him.

He spotted my voice. "Who is it, Mike?"

"It is just what you think it is. It is a witch from outer space."

That stumped him, and he left us alone. They were starting to get lined up anyway.

We got in line, and the parade began. As we walked around the green, I could hear Bill muttering. I figured he was telling the others what was going on. He must have had a walkie-talkie. We walked past the judges' stand in a single file so they could look us over carefully. Then they talked together for a few minutes.

"We now have the four winners," Mr.

Thomas, the minister, said. "When you hear your costume called please come forward to collect your prize."

An upside-down lady and a scarecrow won the prizes for the funniest costumes. They went to the stage and got their prizes. They took off their masks, so everyone could see who they were. It was Eileen Brown and Jim Chapman.

"Now for the most original costumes," the minister said. "These prizes go to the skyscraper and the witch from outer space."

"Holy smoke," I said. "What are we going to do? You won't be able to take off your mask. Beat it."

Bill tried to move away, but the children kept pushing him forward. He had no choice but to go to the platform.

The skyscraper took off his box and col-
lected his prize. The minister handed Bill his
prize and then said, "Would you take off your
mask so we can see who you are?"

Then something strange happened. It started to rain.

"Quickly," the minister called. "Everyone into the Sunday School room."

Everyone started running, and in the confusion I saw Bill slip away. It was too bad that he couldn't attend the party, but he wouldn't have enjoyed it anyway. How could you duck for apples and eat ice cream and cake if you couldn't take off your space helmet?

I found out later that he won a Boy Scout canteen.

4. Space Reports

I was in the swamp right after breakfast. They asked me questions most of the day, but let me go home for lunch. By five o'clock I was pretty worn out.

"You have been wonderful," one said. "When we return in two years we hope to see

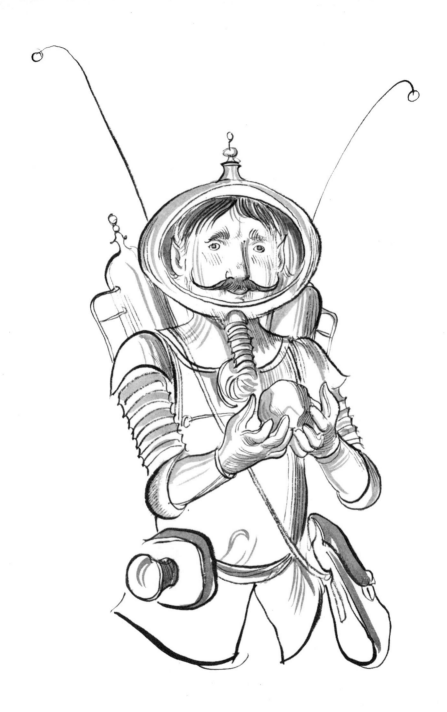

you again. Our visit next time will be official."

"Let someone know you are coming. Maybe you should call the President in Washington. You would be very welcome. They have red carpets for people like you."

"It is hoped that you will tell them about our visit and our plans for returning. Please tell them that we are friendly." I nodded. "We have been trying to figure out what to give you for your services. The only thing we have is a piece of kepto. It is worth a great deal on Barko." He gave me a green-colored stone about the size of a baseball.

"Thank you," I said. "I'll try and get in touch with Washington and tell them about you."

We shook hands, and they started for the

spaceship. "We won't leave until you get home safely. Tell your family the whole story. Good-by."

"Good-by," I said, and started for home.

Both Mom and Dad were in the living room when I got there. Dad was listening to the football scores on television and Mom was knitting.

"Where have you been all day?" she asked.

"I can explain everything now," I said. "I have been with a..." I wasn't sure the words would come out, but out they came "...a spaceship." Good. They had gone.

"A spaceship," Dad said. "What kind of nonsense is that." And he turned back to the television set.

"Please listen to me," I shouted. "It's important!"

"Ted," my mother said calmly to my father, "I think we had better listen. He is quite upset."

Dad turned off the television set, and I told them the whole story. At the end I showed him the stone.

"I've never seen anything like it before. It may be worth some money." He showed it to my mother. "What do you think, Sue?"

"He has been acting strange the last few days," Mom said. "And *he* certainly seems convinced."

"I think I'll run next door and show it to Fred Scott. He used to be a geologist."

The rest of the weekend was taken up by

writing the story you have just read. But that wasn't the end of it. Mr. Scott said that he'd never seen or read about anything like the stone. Then, my dad called Washington and spoke to someone who asked to see my paper. I got it back from Miss Rose, and the next week we were called to Washington for an interview.

I'm sorry but I can't write or tell too much about the Pentagon. That is *Very Top Secret*, even today. All I can say is that they asked a lot of questions, and I had to draw pictures of the men and the ship. I was classified *Top Secret*. They made me promise not to write or say anything about the spaceship for two years. I was blocked again, but so were my mom and dad.

I don't think Washington really believed me. They had to report all this to someone in Colorado who was taking charge of U.F.O.'s. They did admit finally that the stone was very unusual and not found anywhere on earth. It was returned to me and is in the bank. I'll use it if I ever go to Barko. They thought the water spilling and the teachers' meeting and the sudden rainstorm were a bit unusual, but could have been just lucky coincidence. I don't believe it.

It has been two years now, and I can tell my story—or anyway, most of it. I don't want publicity. That is not my point. The spaceship should be coming back soon, and they only have the maps from the atlas to guide them. They may not find Washington, or be able to get in touch with the President. The point is that we should be on the lookout for them. They really are nice people.